Dear Parents and Educators,

Welcome to Penguin Young Readers! As parents and educators, you know that each child develops at his or her own pace—in terms of speech, critical thinking, and, of course, reading. Penguin Young Readers recognizes this fact. As a result, each Penguin Young Readers book is assigned a traditional easy-to-read level (1–4) as well as a Guided Reading Level (A–P). Both of these systems will help you choose the right book for your child. Please refer to the back of each book for specific leveling information. Penguin Young Readers features esteemed authors and illustrators, stories about favorite characters, fascinating nonfiction, and more!

Strawberry Shortcake™
A Brand-New Look!

LEVEL 2

GUIDED READING LEVEL **G**

This book is perfect for a **Progressing Reader** who:
- can figure out unknown words by using picture and context clues;
- can recognize beginning, middle, and ending sounds;
- can make and confirm predictions about what will happen in the text; and
- can distinguish between fiction and nonfiction.

Here are some **activities** you can do during and after reading this book:
- Problem/Solution: In this story, Orange Blossom makes a lot of mistakes. This is the problem. Discuss the solution to the problem. Then talk about another problem in the story and its solution.
- Character's Feelings: Orange has many experiences in the story and feels differently during each one. Discuss how she feels during the following scenes:
  - When she makes mistakes at the store
  - When Mr. Longface Caterpillar tells her his idea
  - When she sees her friends dressed sillily

Remember, sharing the love of reading with a child is the best gift you can give!

—Bonnie Bader, EdM
  Penguin Young Readers program

*Penguin Young Readers are leveled by independent reviewers applying the standards developed by Irene Fountas and Gay Su Pinnell in *Matching Books to Readers: Using Leveled Books in Guided Reading*, Heinemann, 1999.

Penguin Young Readers
Published by the Penguin Group
Penguin Group (USA) Inc., 375 Hudson Street, New York, New York 10014, USA
Penguin Group (Canada), 90 Eglinton Avenue East, Suite 700, Toronto, Ontario M4P 2Y3, Canada
(a division of Pearson Penguin Canada Inc.)
Penguin Books Ltd, 80 Strand, London WC2R 0RL, England
Penguin Ireland, 25 St Stephen's Green, Dublin 2, Ireland (a division of Penguin Books Ltd)
Penguin Group (Australia), 707 Collins Street, Melbourne, Victoria 3008,
Australia (a division of Pearson Australia Group Pty Ltd)
Penguin Books India Pvt Ltd, 11 Community Centre, Panchsheel Park, New Delhi—110 017, India
Penguin Group (NZ), 67 Apollo Drive, Rosedale, Auckland 0632, New Zealand
(a division of Pearson New Zealand Ltd)
Penguin Books, Rosebank Office Park, 181 Jan Smuts Avenue, Parktown North 2193,
South Africa Penguin China, B7 Jaiming Center, 27 East Third Ring Road North,
Chaoyang District, Beijing 100020, China

Penguin Books Ltd., Registered Offices: 80 Strand, London WC2R 0RL, England

Strawberry Shortcake™ and related trademarks © 2013 Those Characters From Cleveland, Inc.
Used under license by Penguin Young Readers Group. All rights reserved. Published by Penguin Young
Readers, an imprint of Penguin Group (USA) Inc., 345 Hudson Street, New York, New York 10014.
Manufactured in China.

ISBN 978-0-448-46280-6   10 9 8 7 6 5 4 3 2 1

Strawberry Shortcake

A Brand-New Look!

by Lana Jacobs
illustrated by MJ Illustrations

Penguin Young Readers
An Imprint of Penguin Group (USA) Inc.

Orange Blossom loves

to work at the store.

She works hard at the store.

Here comes Strawberry Shortcake.

She needs new dishes for her café.

Orange sees the dishes

over there.

Oh no!

The dishes are not where

Orange said they would be.

Orange did not see the dishes.
The dishes were right in
front of her.

Look!

Here comes Lemon Meringue.

See how many things

she needs to buy!

Uh-oh!

Orange made a mistake.

Orange could not read

the prices.

Orange did not add up

Lemon's things the right way.

Now Orange has to start all over.

14

Orange is sad.

Why does she keep making mistakes?

Mr. Longface Caterpillar
has an idea.

Orange is making mistakes

because she cannot see.

Orange needs glasses!

Orange does not want glasses.

What will her friends think?

Strawberry sees Orange.

Orange looks sad.

Orange tells Strawberry

she needs glasses.

Strawberry tries to

make her feel better.

But Orange still looks sad.

Strawberry has an idea!

She cannot wait to tell

her friends.

They will work together

to help Orange.

Raspberry gives everyone
new clothes.

Lemon gives everyone
funny hairdos.

Now the girls look really silly.

It is time to go see Orange!

Orange smiles when

she sees Raspberry.

Raspberry looks so silly!

Orange smiles when

she sees Strawberry.

Strawberry looks so silly!

Orange understands the game
the girls are playing.

They are not friends with Orange
because of how she looks.

They are friends with her

because she is a good friend.

Orange is happy now.

She is ready to get glasses!